USBORNE FIRST READING

The Dinosaur Who Lost His ROAR

Russell Punter
Illustrated by Andy Elkerton

USBORNE FIRST READING

The Castle That Jack Built

Lesley Sims
Illustrated by
Mike Gordon

USBORNE FIRST READING

Chicken Licken

retold by
Russell Punter
Illustrated by Ann Kronheimer

USBORNE FIRST READING

The Three Little Pigs

retold by
Susanna Davidson
Illustrated by Georgien Overwater

The Fish that Talked

Retold by Rosie Dickins

Illustrated by
Graham Philpot

Reading Consultant: Alison Kelly
Roehampton University

Long ago, in India, there was
a young man named Manu.

One day, Manu was
wading in a stream.

4

A tiny fish swam into
his hands.

The fish sparkled with a
silvery light.

6

"Help!" it said. "The big fish want to eat me."

It talks!

7

"Poor little thing,"
said Manu.

He cupped his
hands and carried
the fish home.

9

He put the fish into a jar
of water...

Splash!

and fed it with crumbs.

It grew...

and grew...

I have no room to swim.

until it was too big for the jar.

11

So Manu took the fish to the well...

Splash!

and fed it with bread.

12

So Manu carried the fish
to the river.

Splash!

He didn't feed
it, but...

15

"Please take me to the sea," begged the fish.

Manu groaned. "He'll weigh a ton," he thought.

But amazingly, the fish
was as light as air.

19

Manu walked to the
seashore and threw the
fish into the sea.

21

"Thank you," said the fish.

You are a good man.

"Now it's my turn to help you."

22

"There is going to be a great flood."

"You must build a boat to save all living things."

So Manu built a
huge boat...

and filled it with plants
and animals.

Soon, dark clouds
filled the sky.

Then, the rain came.

27

It rained and rained, until
water covered the land.

Only Manu's boat floated
above the waves.

The wind howled and waves crashed around the boat.

"We must find shelter,"
said Manu, "or we'll sink!"

He peered into the dark...
and saw a silvery light.

It was the talking fish.

Throw me a rope.

The fish pulled the boat through the storm. After a long, long time, they reached a great mountain.

Its top rose out of the
flood like an island.

Suddenly, the fish changed...

"I am Brahma,* lord of all creatures," it said.

* Say **Braa**-*muh*

Manu gasped. Brahma
was a powerful god.

"I have saved you so you can rebuild the world."

"And you, Manu, will be its king."

"Rule wisely!"
said Brahma.

"I will," promised Manu.

Brahma vanished in a
flash of silvery light.

Manu never saw Brahma again. But he never forgot what the god said.

After the flood, he worked
hard to rebuild the world.

And he ruled wisely and
well for the rest of his days.

45

About this story

The Fish that Talked comes from an ancient Indian poem called *The Mahabharata,** which tells of gods and men and war. The original poem is 18 books long and over 2,000 years old.

In some versions, it is the Hindu god Vishnu who takes the form of the fish that grew and grew and saved the world.

* Say *Muh-har-**bar**-uh-tuh*

USBORNE FIRST READING
Level Four

USBORNE FIRST READING

The Dragon Painter

retold by
Rosie Dickins
Illustrated by John Nez

USBORNE FIRST READING

The Ugly Duckling

based on the story by
Hans Christian Andersen
Illustrated by Daniel Postgate

USBORNE FIRST READING

The RUNAWAY PANCAKE

retold by
Mairi Mackinnon
Illustrated by
Silvia Provantini

USBORNE FIRST READING

Little Red Riding Hood

based on the story by The Brothers Grimm
Illustrated by Mike Gordon